Bedtime Bunnies

WORDS AND PICTURES BY **Wendy Watson**

CLARION BOOKS
Houghton Mifflin Harcourt
Boston • New York

Clarion Books

215 Park Avenue South, New York, New York 10003

Copyright © 2010 by Wendy Watson

The illustrations were executed in pencil, watercolors,
and acrylics on hot press watercolor paper.
The text was set in Billy Light.

Clarion Books is an imprint of Houghton Mifflin Harcourt Publishing Company.

www.hmhbooks.com

Manufactured in China

Library of Congress Cataloging-in-Publication Data
Watson, Wendy.
Bedtime bunnies / story and pictures by Wendy Watson.
p. cm.
Summary: Bunnies scamper, scurry, splash, zip, and snuggle as they get ready for bed.
ISBN 978-0-547-22312-4
[1. Bedtime—Fiction. 2. Rabbits—Fiction.] I. Title.
PZ7.W332Be 2011
[E]—dc22   2009047726

LEO 10 9 8 7 6 5 4 3
4500283064

Bedtime Bunnies

For Elizabeth

Bedtime, Bunnies!

Hop

Sip
Slurp
Guzzle
Gulp

Squirt Scrub Splutter Spit

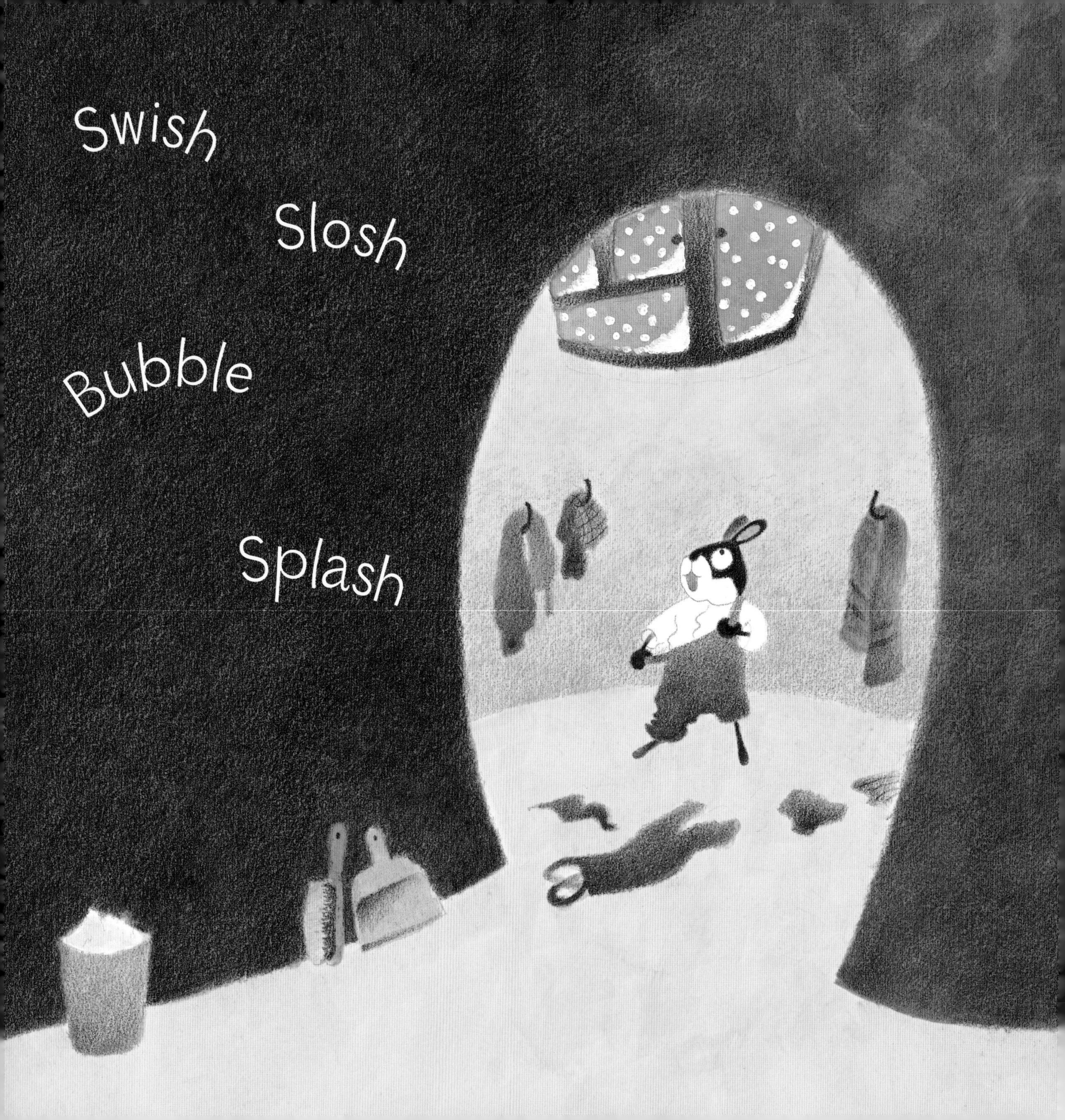
Swish
Slosh
Bubble
Splash

Pop

Zip

Button   Snap

Snuggle   Squeeze

Dearie   Darling

Cuddle   Hug

Quiet

Shush

Hush

Shhh

Good night, bunnies.

*To Enzo mio
and his dream*

Patricia Lee Gauch, Editor

200 Madison Avenue, New York, NY 10016. Philomel Books, Reg. U.S. Pat. & Tm. Off.
Published simultaneously in Canada. Printed in Hong Kong by South China
Printing Co. (1988) Ltd. Book design by Donna Mark. The text is set in Administer Book.
Library of Congress Cataloging-in-Publication Data. Polacco, Patricia. In Enzo's splendid gardens /
Patricia Polacco. p. cm.   Summary: A cumulative rhyme describes the uproarious chain of events that
ensue when a waiter trips over a book dropped by a boy watching a bee. [1. Restaurants—Fiction.
2. Stories in rhyme.] I. Title. PZ8.3.P55895In 1997 [E]—dc20 96-12360 CIP AC
3 4 5 6 7 8 9 10   ISBN 0-399-23107-2

In Enzo's Splendid Gardens

PATRICIA POLACCO

Philomel Books   New York

This is the bee that stopped on a tree in Enzo's splendid gardens.

Here is the boy who dropped his book as
he turned around to take a good look
at the fuzzy old bee, just there on the tree
in Enzo's splendid gardens.

Here is the waiter who tipped his tray, who otherwise
would have had a good day, but tripped
on the edge of the little boy's book;
he'd just turned 'round to take a good look
at that fuzzy old bee, there on the tree
in Enzo's splendid gardens.

This is the matron, all dressed in pink, on whose
bodice was splashed a very large drink, tipped
from the tray, on a very bad day,
by the waiter who fell over the book, dropped
by the boy who turned 'round to look
at that funny old bee, there on the tree
in Enzo's splendid gardens.

These are the ladies, foo-foo and shee-shee, who lost
their balance and spilled their tea, bumped
by the matron, all dressed in pink, on whose
bodice was splashed a very large drink, tipped
from the tray, on a horrible day, by the waiter who fell
over the book, dropped by the boy who turned 'round
to look at that silly old bee, there on the tree
in Enzo's splendid gardens.

Here is the man who fell on the cart where all
the desserts were fine works of art, pushed
by the ladies, foo-foo and shee-shee, who lost
their balance and spilled their tea, bumped
by the matron, all dressed in pink, on whose
bodice was splashed a very large drink, tipped
from the tray—an awful day!—by the waiter who fell
over the book dropped by the boy who turned 'round
to look at that crazy old bee, there on the tree
in Enzo's splendid gardens.

Here is the chef, who heard the commotion, who
jostled a pot and set it in motion by running
to help the man on the cart, who now was covered
in lovely fruit tarts, pushed
by the ladies, foo-foo and shee-shee, who lost
their balance and spilled their tea,
bumped by the matron, all dressed in pink,
on whose bodice was splashed a very large drink, tipped
from the tray—a dreadful day!—by the waiter who fell
over the book dropped by the boy who turned 'round
to look at that sunny old bee, there on the tree
in Enzo's splendid gardens.

Here comes Enzo, full of spaghetti, chasing
his cat, whose name is Lettie, hoping to catch her,
but she thinks not and runs through the room,
wearing the pot that was jostled and spilled
and set into motion by the chef, who heard all
the commotion, who ran to help the man on the
cart, covered and smothered in edible art,
pushed by the ladies, foo-foo and shee-shee, who
lost their balance and spilled their tea, bumped
by the matron, all dressed in pink, on whose
bodice was splashed a very large drink, tipped
from the tray—nasty ol' day!—by the waiter who fell
over the book dropped by the boy who turned 'round
to look at that smug old bee, there on the tree
in Enzo's splendid gardens.

Here are the diners who all rushed to see, and
started to laugh and relish with glee, Enzo still
running, hurling spaghetti, trying to catch poor
little Lettie. She was hissing and spitting and
howling a lot; she ran out the door, wearing
the pot that was jostled and spilled and set into motion
by the chef, who heard all the commotion, who
ran to help the man on the cart, oozing and
gooey in flavorful art, pushed
by the ladies, foo-foo and shee-shee, who
lost their balance and spilled their tea, bumped
by the matron, all dressed in pink,
on whose bodice was splashed a very large drink, tipped
from the tray—horrible day!—by the waiter who fell
over the book dropped by the boy who turned 'round
to look at that chuckling bee, there on the tree
in Enzo's splendid gardens.

These are the dishes that hit the floor as all the
patrons dashed out the door, laughing and catching
Enzo's spaghetti; it tangled and twisted 'round
poor little Lettie. Hissing and spitting, her legs
in a knot, she stumbled and climbed, still wearing that
pot that was jostled and spilled and set into motion
by the chef, who saw and heard the commotion, who
ran to help the man on the cart, with chocolate and
pies stuck to his heart, pushed by the ladies, foo-foo
and shee-shee, who lost their balance and spilled
their tea, bumped by the matron, all dressed in pink,
on whose bodice was splashed that very large
drink, tipped from the tray—ghastly ol' day!—
by the waiter who fell over the book
dropped by the boy who turned 'round to look
at that bumbling bee, there on the tree
in Enzo's splendid gardens.

There is Sam, climbing the palm, for Lettie ran
up it and won't come down. Enzo was gasping, the
crowd held its breath; if either should fall it would
surely mean death. The crowd tried to rope her,
they tied a great knot, then down with a crash
came the old pot that was jostled and spilled
and set into motion by the chef, who saw and
heard the commotion, who ran to help the man
on the cart, completely consumed in sweet
tasty art, pushed by the ladies, foo-foo and shee-shee,
who lost their balance and spilled their tea, bumped
by the matron, all dressed in pink, on whose bodice
was splashed that very large drink, tipped from
the tray—man, what a day!—by the waiter who fell
over that book, dropped by the boy who turned 'round
to look at that daring old bee, still on the tree
in Enzo's splendid gardens.

This is the engine, one twenty-six, led by the chief they all called "Big Mick." They roared up in front and put on their hats; they climbed up that palm and rescued that cat! The fire chief smiled and seemed in good cheer, but then he asked, "Who brought us here?"

"I tripped on something, there by the door," the
waiter called out as he looked at the floor.
"You found it, it's mine!" Then all turned to look
at the boy. "Yes, it's mine. It's my favorite book!

"I tripped on that book, it made me fall. I tipped the tray and spilled the drink that fell on the matron, all dressed in pink, who bumped the ladies, foo-foo and shee-shee, who lost their balance and upset their tea, who pushed the man who fell on the cart, still covered in pudding, eating a tart. Then the chef came running, steaming and hot, and pushed over the gurgling pot that was full to the brim with loads of spaghetti, which flipped and flopped and fell on poor Lettie, who ran through the room and caused the commotion that set these events in terrible motion."

The little boy said, "Then I guess it was me!
All I was doin' was watchin' a bee. Who knew
that he'd stop and land on that tree
in Enzo's splendid gardens?"